JIM SILKE'S RASCALS IN PARADISE™

series editor BOB SCHRECK
collection editor LYNN ADAIR
collection designer CARY GRAZZINI
collection design manager BRIAN GOGOLIN

Special thanks to Dave Stevens for his expert advice and encouragement, and to Sam Peckinpah, Brigitte Bardot, Claudia Cardinale, Maureen O'Sullivan, Toshiro Mifune, and Victor McLaglen for their inspiration.

This book collects issues one through three
of the Dark Horse comic-book series *Rascals in Paradise*™.

Published by Dark Horse Comics
10956 SE Main Street
Milwaukie, OR 97222

First edition: November 1995
ISBN: 1-56971-075-9

Limited edition
ISBN: 1-56971-141-0

10 9 8 7 6 5 4 3 2 1

PRINTED IN CANADA

RASCALS IN PARADISE™

story and art by

JIM SILKE

lettered by **L. LOIS BUHALIS**

introductions by **DAVE STEVENS** *and* **GEOF DARROW**

A LYN & JIM HOT CHOCOLATE PRODUCTION

TWO EASY PIECES

A Few Words About the Rascal Behind Rascals

IF YOU'VE ALREADY FLIPPED THROUGH THE PAGES of *Rascals in Paradise*, chances are that you've also come to a pretty obvious conclusion. That is: Jim Silke *loves* dramatic close-ups. But unfortunately for the *male* characters in this serial, *they* weren't given any! At least, it sure seems that way to this reader. Okay, so Silke threw String and Sam a few small, halfhearted head shots . . . big deal!

We know that if he'd stopped long enough to think about it, he'd have probably found a way to write *out* all those pesky male characters cluttering up the scenery in his personal little parable of pulchritude. The *dames* are the thing here! (Or am I overstating the obvious? I think so.)

Oh, he may stomp his feet and wave his arms about this being his tribute to some of his favorite films from Hollywood's Golden Age, but *we* know different, don't we? We know that, in his heart of hearts, he's really in the front row of the Red Garter Room, squinting through opera glasses in one hand and brandishing a shaky pen and pad in the other. ("It's only for research!" Yes, Silke, we know the song.)

I think he protests too much.

You see, ever since his glory days as an eager-beaver young art director at Capitol Records, he's found a way to play out his feverish fascination with the fairer sex, even if only on paper, the most memorable being his photo covers and layouts for the gone but not forgotten *Cinema* magazine, for which he also edited and provided numerous interviews. He also found time to illustrate scores of articles for men's magazines in the early 1960s, as well as to interview and photograph nearly *every* famous and not-so-famous actress and ingenue of the entire decade! I could go on here, but what's the point? It's too painful!

Fast forward to 1995. Here he is, thirty years older, a bit wiser. You'd think after all that, *and* becoming a successful screenwriter, working with the likes of Sam Peckinpah, George Stevens, and others, that he'd just about done it all. Right? Uh-uh. Now, of all things, he wants to do a comic book! Entirely by the seat of his pants, yet. And what's he going to put in it? Of course: (all together now) *dames*! Full-page, glorious studies in radiant colors, calling to mind such sultry beauties a Claudia Cardinale and Bebe Bardot. All beautifully posed and dramatically lit, with smouldering eyes and pouting lips — ye gods! The nerve of this guy!

So, what's the point, Stevens? There is no point, other than I'm jealous as hell of the career he's had, the cinematic giants he's known (Ford, Stevens, Hitchcock, Truffaut, etc.), the actresses he's — ahh! Enough, already!

And to top it off, he now has this great, first-time attempt at comics, with more pages and better reproduction than I've *ever* had. What's worse is that he's committed, disciplined, and talented as all get out!

Just *who* does he think he is, anyway . . . Some kinda boy genius? *Grow up, Silke! Act your age!*

You'll all have to excuse me now. I'm going out to the back yard, to eat worms.

—Dave Stevens
Studio City, California
1995

I SUPPOSE THE BEST WAY FOR ME TO BEGIN is to give an account of how I was first introduced to Jim Silke. As it does for so many of today's social problems, the blame falls on Dave Stevens.

Every year at the San Diego Comics Convention, I used to pass as much time as possible close to Dave Stevens' booth because of all the amazing conversations I could overhear. There'd be industrial designers seeking Dave's advice on the perfect shape and design of panty liners and assorted feminine products; various law-enforcement types trying to see if Dave could identify the owner of an odd pasty or G-string by size or odor, taken from a crime scene; or a heated debate over zero-gravity situation. Dave, in his usual polite, casual form, would give each inquiry serious and deliberate consideration and then provide an answer that I'd note and use to frighten the folks back home on holidays. This was a constant at Dave's booth.

One other constant was a tall, lanky, blue-jeaned guy who'd drift in every year and settle near Dave to show, what from my discreet vantage point seemed to be, a selection of drawings. That guy was Jim Silke. I didn't notice Jim's work at first because there was an odd familiarity about him that haunted me. I'd study his features, ignoring to my gross stupidity, the brilliant figure work, design, and color sense fanned out before Dave. Each year, I'd rack my brain to solve my self-created riddle: *What was it about Jim Silke's face?* Jim would very modestly be discussing with Dave his experience in film as designer, art director, or writer, or his encounters with the greatest cineasts the world would ever know: Ford, Hawks, Hitchcock; and I'd be over in some corner ignoring the amazing world of knowledge available to the hungry ear at large wondering, *what is it about this Silke guy*?

Years later, it hit me. Whether it was a specific phrase or the way he mouthed something that triggered it, I don't know, but I finally had it! *It was his lips! I knew them.* They'd been an important part of my childhood. Every fundamental piece of information — moral or technical — I then held to be true and which now make up my day-to-day consciousness, had been imparted to me by those lips. Yes, Jim Silke's lips had been the lips of Clutch Cargo! That everyman, that animated role model that every child of the '60s held to highest esteem, Clark Haas' demigod of virtue and justice brought to further life by the addition of Jim Silke's own lips.

When I'd been formerly introduced to Jim, I confided to him that I was aware of his important part in animated and social history. Jim neither admitted nor denied being Clutch's spokesman. But the smile that tugged at those oh, so expressive lips was all the answer I needed. Maybe he'd signed a vow of eternal silence or was afraid of the notoriety and the sure-to-follow clamor for public appearances and lip prints from fans. I'll never know, but it's been a pleasure for me to finally meet Clutch's lips.

As important as Jim's lips were to Clutch Cargo's success and his subsequent impact on society, the book you now hold in your hands overshadows even that. In *Rascals in Paradise*, Jim has given readers his all. From words to pictures, it's all Jim. He doesn't treat his public like dolts; he gives from heart and mind, a perfect combination. I thank God there are still artists like Jim, willing to give his audience a read they can enjoy and respect and not dispose of, unlike so much in the comics market today.

So if you've just bought *Rascals* and, like me, are struggling through this rambling introduction, sit back. It's almost over, and you're about to spend some time in the company of one of the nicest, most talented men I've ever met!

P.S. I'm still sure Jim's lips were Clutch Cargo's lips, and I've suspicions that Mike Richardson's lips were Spinner's lips, Spinner being Clutch's young charge.

—Geof Darrow
La Caine, France
1995

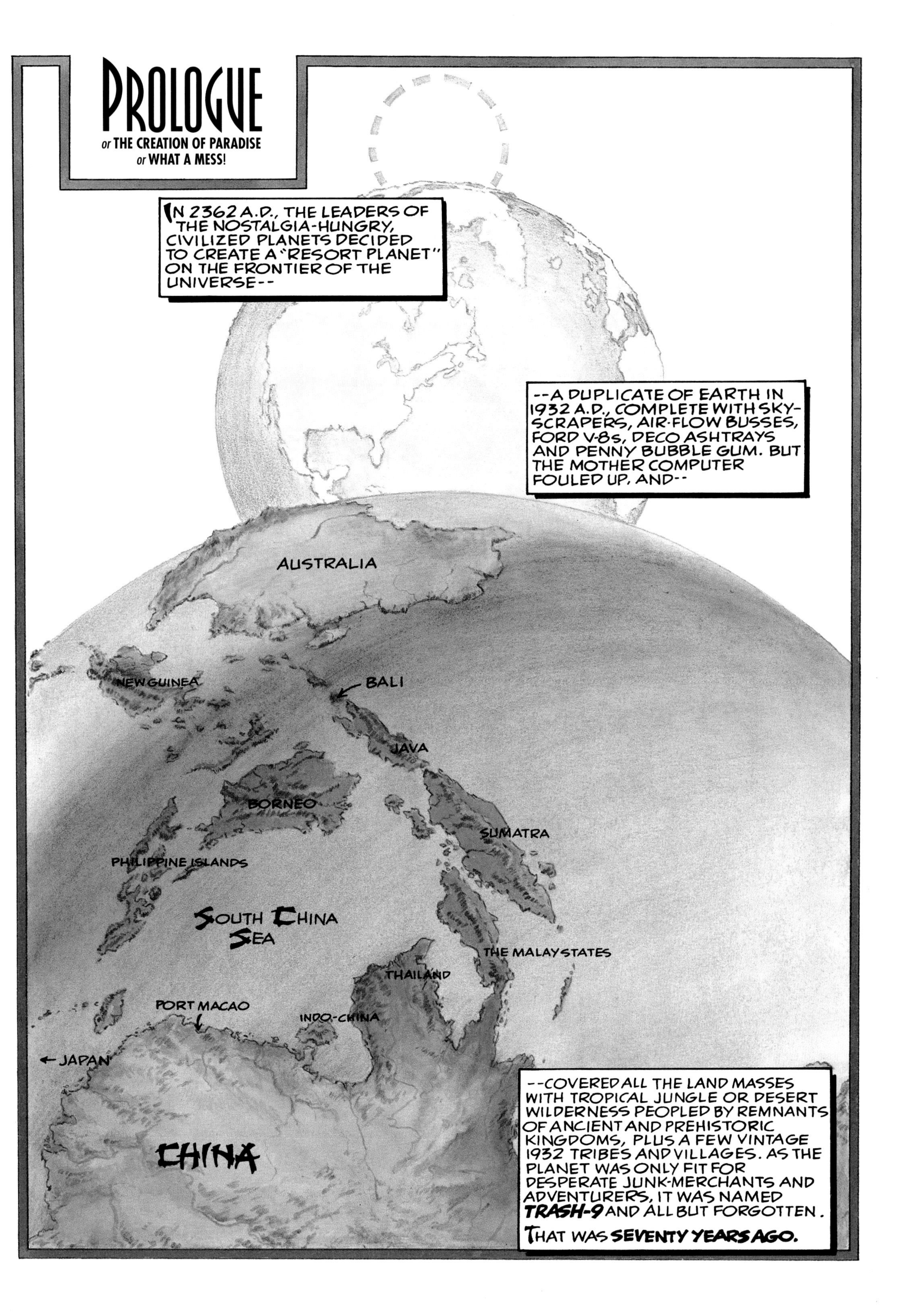
PROLOGUE
or THE CREATION OF PARADISE
or WHAT A MESS!
IN 2362 A.D., THE LEADERS OF THE NOSTALGIA-HUNGRY, CIVILIZED PLANETS DECIDED TO CREATE A "RESORT PLANET" ON THE FRONTIER OF THE UNIVERSE--
--A DUPLICATE OF EARTH IN 1932 A.D., COMPLETE WITH SKY-SCRAPERS, AIR-FLOW BUSSES, FORD V-8s, DECO ASHTRAYS AND PENNY BUBBLE GUM. BUT THE MOTHER COMPUTER FOULED UP, AND--
AUSTRALIA
NEW GUINEA
BALI
JAVA
BORNEO
SUMATRA
PHILIPPINE ISLANDS
SOUTH CHINA SEA
THE MALAY STATES
THAILAND
PORT MACAO
INDO-CHINA
← JAPAN
CHINA
--COVERED ALL THE LAND MASSES WITH TROPICAL JUNGLE OR DESERT WILDERNESS PEOPLED BY REMNANTS OF ANCIENT AND PREHISTORIC KINGDOMS, PLUS A FEW VINTAGE 1932 TRIBES AND VILLAGES. AS THE PLANET WAS ONLY FIT FOR DESPERATE JUNK-MERCHANTS AND ADVENTURERS, IT WAS NAMED TRASH-9 AND ALL BUT FORGOTTEN.
THAT WAS SEVENTY YEARS AGO.

EPISODE 1

THE WOMAN RACKET

THURSDAY, MAY 19, 2432. FROM A STRANGE EDIFICE HIDDEN DEEP IN THE MALAY JUNGLE, THREE SAVAGES DEPART BEARING SHACKLES AND CHAINS.
DAYS LATER, THEIR SHADOWS FALL ACROSS A MOONLIT STREET OUTSIDE THE BLUE PARROT NIGHTCLUB IN PORT MACAO, TRASH -9'S LONE OUTPOST OF CIVILIZATION.
INSIDE, ROGUE ADVENTURERS, JUNK MERCHANTS, OUTLAWS, AND RECLAMATION BULLDOGS GREET THE NEW ACT AS--
--ONE OF THE SAVAGES PEERS THROUGH A WINDOW TO STUDY--

JANE "THE FRISCO FIRE," MAXWELL IN HER DEBUT PERFORMANCE ON TRASH-9.
THE MUSIC TURNS HOT AND HEADY, JANE GOES WITH IT, AND--
O.K., KID! ENOUGH OF THE CUTE STUFF!! IF YOU'RE SO ALL FIRED HOT--
--PROVE IT!
YEAH! BRECKENRIDGE'S RIGHT! PEEL!!! FLASH THOSE HEADLIGHTS!
PEEL!! HEADLIGHTS!
YOU HEARD THEM, SOFT ONE--SHOW ME YOURS IS THE SACRED FLESH--PROVE IT!
STRIP! STRIP! STRIP! STRIP! STRIP!
NOOOOOOOOOOO
STOP HER!!
IT'S TOO LATE TA RUN, KID!
YESSSS! TOO LATE!! GRAB HER!

SIMMER DOWN, BOYS--THE SHOW'S **OVER!**
STRING! THANK **GOD!!!**
JAMES LOWELL STRINGFELLOW, RECRUITING SERGEANT OF THE **CHRYSLER RIFLES,** THE LAW ON TRASH-9.

OUT OF THE WAY, SOLDIER!
NOBODY'S PAYING YOU TO BE HER **LOOKOUT!** **SHE'S FAIR GAME!**

I'M AFRAID, GENTLEMEN, YOU'RE **WRONG**. MISS MAXWELL IS NOW UNDER THE REGIMENT'S PROTECTION.

EASE OFF, BOYS. IT SEEMS THE SERGEANT IS TAKING THIS A SHADE "PERSONAL," AN WE GOT BETTER THINGS TO DO.
YEAH!! WE GOT **BETTER** THINGS TO DO!
OKAY, STRING! **TAKE** YOUR BIMBO!! BUT YOU OWE US!

MOVE IT, JANE! BRECKENRIDGE TENDS TO CHANGE HIS MIND!
I'M COMING! I'M COMING!
GALLANTLY DONE, HANDSOME ONE--IT'S A **PITY** YOU'RE SUCH A DANGEROUS NUISANCE!

LATER, THE SAVAGES MEET SECRETLY AT A DESERTED VILLAGE GATE.
SHE FAILED TO REMOVE HER CLOTHING--WE MUST STEAL HER.
BUT MASTER-- IN THE LAIR OF THE RIFLES!? BUT--BUT SHE MIGHT BE THE WRONG ONE!
I HAVE NO CHOICE!!
RRRRRR-RRR
HEAR THAT? EVEN THE BEASTS GROW IMPATIENT. HURRY! THE LIGHTED WINDOW IS HERS.
AT THE SAME MOMENT, INSIDE--
I BLEW IT, DIDN'T I, STRING? BUT DON'T FIRE ME! THOSE BRUTES WOULD SCARE ANYONE! JUST GIVE ME ANOTHER CHANCE AND I'LL DO EVERYTHING THE WAY YOU TAUGHT ME. EVERY STEP!
I SURELY HOPE SO. YOU'RE A DIFFERENT GIRL THAN THE ONE WHO GOT OFF THE AIR-BUS FIVE WEEKS AGO--AND ONCE YOU ADMIT IT, WE'LL BOTH BE IN THE GRAVY.
I GUESS YOU'RE RIGHT-- I HAVE CHANGED. EVERYTHING'S SO STRANGE ON THIS PLANET! SO SAVAGE AND SENSUAL-- IT MAKES ME WANT TO DO THINGS!
THAT'S NOT THE PLANET, DUMPLING, THAT'S ME!
Shhhh-- NOTHING'S GOING TO HAPPEN TO YOU WHILE I'M AROUND! Ummm!
Oh, STRING, YES! BUT--

OH!! STRING!
RELAX! IT'S JUST THE GENERATORS AGAIN.
BUT I SMELL PERFUME! AND IT'S NOT MINE!
EEEEE
THAT'S HER!! MOVE!!
HOLD IT RIGHT THERE!
WHISH
LOOK OUT!
THUD!
NO!
SILENCE HER!! SHE'LL SUMMON HER POWERS!

THE CHAINS! **QUICK!**
NOW TAKE HER OUT THE WINDOW. **HURRY! HURRY!**
OH, **GOD!** I SHOULD **NEVER** HAVE GOTTEN OFF THAT **AIRBUS!!**
COME ON, EYES, OPEN!
PLEASE, **NOOooo**
SO, SERGEANT, YOU STILL WISH TO BE A PLAYER IN THE **GREAT GAME!** WELL, WE WILL SEE.
IS THAT MY **GUN??** I THINK THAT'S MY GUN.

DON'T WORRY, JANE. THEY'RE HISTORY.
SLEEP WELL, SERGEANT.
STOP!! HE'S HARMLESS NOW--AND HE MAY PROVE--
--AMUSING.
DAWN--STRING AWAKENS TO AN OLD FAMILIAR REFRAIN.
SO, MOONLIGHTIN' AGAIN, WERE YA?
CORK IT, McCHESNEY! THIS TIME THEY STOLE JANE!
AY! AN' THIS TIME I'M TAKIN' THE REGIMENT AFTER 'EM!

IT'S ABOUT TIME! I'LL GET MY GEAR!
NO, YOU WON'T!! FIVE RECRUITS ARE COMIN' IN ON TODAY'S AIRBUS, AN' YER GONNA MEET IT. STAY HERE-- AN' GUARD THE PORT!
OH, NO, McCHESNEY! YOU'RE NOT LEAVIN' ME BEHIND!! I GOT JANE IN THIS MESS-- AN' I'M GETTIN' HER OUT!
STOP WORRYIN'! I'LL FETCH HER FOR YA!
CHRYSLER RIFLES
SLING YER WEAPONS! COLUMN LEFT! FORWARD 'ARCH!
McCHESNEY! I'M WARNING YOU! ONCE YOU MARCH INTO THAT JUNGLE-- I'M OUTTA HERE!
HA!
DON'T MAKE ME LAUGH!
TWO DAYS LATER, AT THE LAGOON LANDING SITE-- STRING AND TWO "BLUE PARROT" HOSTESSES STILL WAIT FOR THE AIRBUS.
RELAX! IT'S DUE ANY MINUTE!
SURE! JUST LIKE YESTERDAY AND THE DAY BEFORE. Groan MY LUCK'S GOTTA CHANGE!
LUCK NOT CHANGE! CARDS SAY FATE MOST HORRIBLE WAITS FOR POOR MISSY JANE.

AT THAT MOMENT, IN THE JUNGLE, ONE OF THE SAVAGES REPORTS TO HIS QUEEN.
SOLDIERS LOSE TRAIL-- SAFE TO STOP NOW.
AT LAST! UNCHAIN HER! PUT HER IN THE LIGHT!
Hmmm! REMOVE HER SLIP! TURN HER AROUND!
GROAN
THERE'S NO MARK ON HER! SHE'S THE WRONG ONE!
THE ONE CALLED BRECKENRIDGE LIED!
YES-- AND HE WILL SUFFER BUT THE GOLD WE PAID FOR HER WILL NOT BE WASTED. WE TAKE HER TO TANIT'S ALTAR.
WE LET BRECK-ENRIDGE GET AWAY?
NO!
HE WON'T RUN. HE'LL BE BUSY-- DOING OUR WORK FOR US.

MEANWHILE, THE MONTHLY AIRBUS FROM EARTH FINALLY ARRIVES--ON BOARD IS--

DORINE 'SPICY' SAUNDERS.
OH, WOW! THERE IT IS! JUST LIKE DAD DESCRIBED IT!!

PORT MACAO
THE MANGROVES FORMING A NATURAL HARBOR-- THE WALLED VILLAGE-- THE RECLAMATION COMPANY'S PRIVATE DOCK-- EVERYTHING!

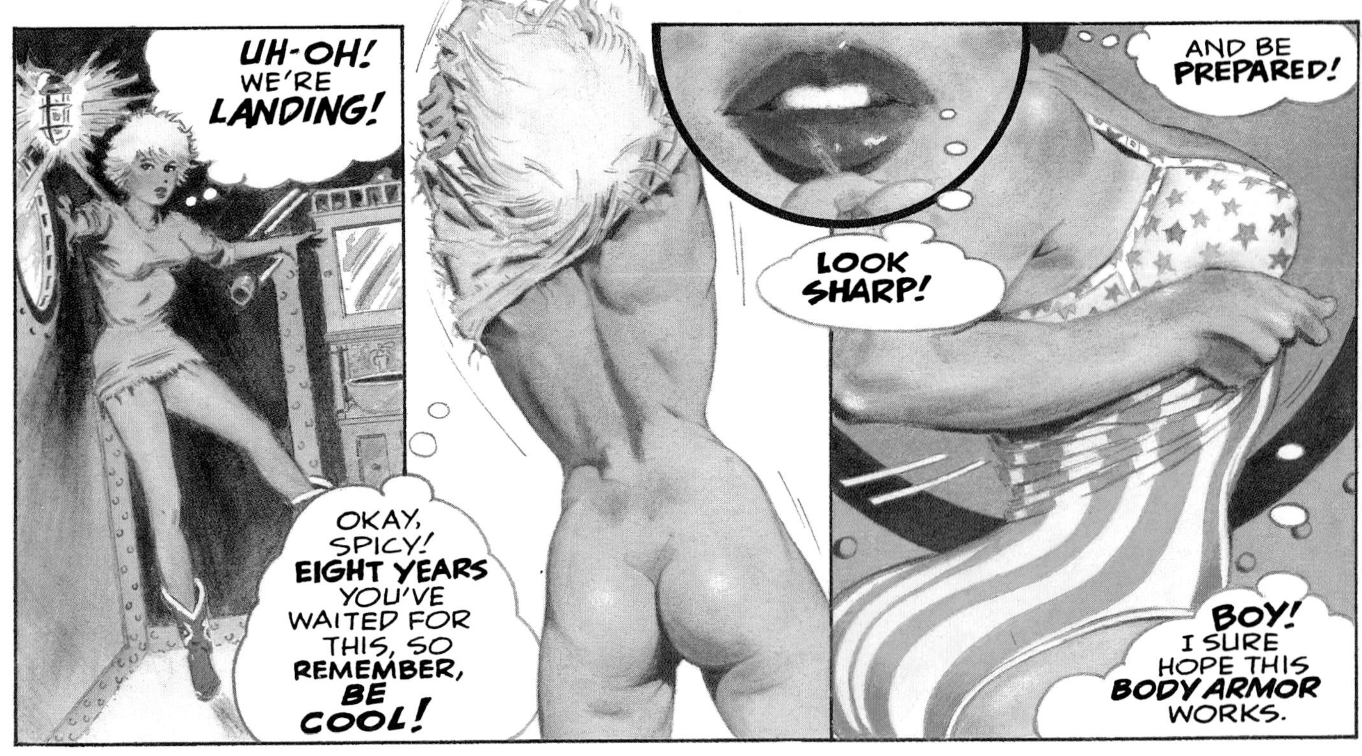
UH-OH! WE'RE LANDING!
OKAY, SPICY! EIGHT YEARS YOU'VE WAITED FOR THIS, SO REMEMBER, BE COOL!
LOOK SHARP!
AND BE PREPARED!
BOY! I SURE HOPE THIS BODY ARMOR WORKS.

OUTSIDE, ON THE BEACH--
LOOK! BANDITS MAKE BUS GO BOOM!
BRECKENRIDGE!
YEAH! I KNEW HE WAS PLANNIN' SOMETHING!
KABOOM!
BLAST THE LIFTERS!
WHAM!
HEY
WHUMP!
SCRAM! STEP ON IT!
YIKE!
YOU BETCHA!

OOPS!!
SCREEE
WHEW!
OH, NO! IT'S ON FIRE!
IT COULD BLOW ANY SECOND!
WITH EVERY-ONE ON BOARD!
UH OH! GOTTA MOVE!
GO AHEAD! TEAR THE WHOLE JUNGLE DOWN! JUST DON'T BLOW!

WHUP
WHOA!
UH OH!
WHRAM
THUNK
SPLATT!!!

OUTSIDE, AT THE LAGOON--
WE'RE CUT OFF!!
SO! SWIM FOR IT!
IF ONLY THE ROCKETS BLEW, THEY COULD STILL BE OKAY!

THE HATCH! SOMEONE'S ALIVE!!
HEY!
YOU OKAY UP THERE?
YOU BET!!
NOW!
WHO DO I SHOOT?

THEY'RE ON THEIR WAY--BUT YOU'RE NOT GOING TO HURT THEM A WHOLE LOT WITH THAT SPOON!

SPOON?! OH, YEAH, I USED IT TO PRY OPEN THE HATCH!

HANG ON!

GREAT! THE LUGGAGE COMPARTMENT'S BEEN BLOWN OPEN. COVER ME-- I'M GOING IN.
HEY! FORGET YOUR LUGGAGE!

WHAT ABOUT THE OTHER PASSENGERS?
THERE AREN'T ANY! JUST ME AND THE DROID PILOTS.

WHAT!! THERE'S SUPPOSED TO BE FIVE RECRUITS ON THIS CRATE!!
SORRY, SARGE. I'M ALL YOU GET.

THEN WE'VE HAD IT. GROAN HERE THEY COME!!

YOU HANDLE STRINGFELLOW! I'LL TAKE THE GIRL!
SURE, SAM! SHE'S ALL YOURS--'LESS, OF COURSE, I GET TO HER FIRST!
YEAH!! 'LESS I GET TO HER FIRST!!
STUFF IT! THIS ISN'T A GAME!
MOVE IT, KID!
WAIT!

NO! MOVE YOUR BUTT!! YOU'VE GOT ONE CHANCE OF STAYING OUT OF A CAGE, AND I'M IT!
I'M COMING! I'M COMING!

WHOOSH
HOLY!!
AWK
TA DA!

CADET SAUNDERS, D., REPORTING FOR DUTY, SARGE. JUST POINT 'EM OUT, AND I'LL BLAST 'EM!
YOU'RE A RECRUIT?! AWWWW NO!

OH, YES! JUST BECAUSE I'M A WOMAN, DON'T--
OOOPS!
THIS BABY'S HEAVY!
THAT'S RIGHT!
I CAN HANDLE IT!
GRUNT
DROP IT, KID. HEAD FOR THE VILLAGE! I'LL COVER YOUR REAR!
NO WAY! THIS IS WHAT I DO!
AAAHHHHHHHHHHHHHH
YEOW!
SHE'LL GET AWAY!
NOT FOR LONG WITH-OUT STRING!
THERE HE IS!!
KPOW POW POW POW

MY GOSH! HE MEANT IT! HE'S DRAWING THEIR FIRE!!

Whoops!
HURRY UP, KID! SCRAM!

DARN!! I'LL SHOW HIM WHO NEEDS RESCUING!!

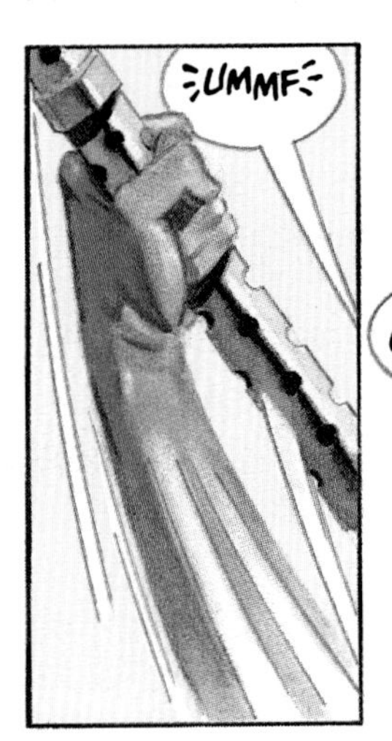
UMMF

GRUNT
Puf!

GOT IT!!

WHA--!!

WHOOSH
WOOOM

ALL RIGHT! THREE DOWN--
--THREE ON THE RUN--

--ONE TO GO!

WHRAM

OUCH!
Hmmmm! IT APPEARS, SERGEANT, YOU'VE FINALLY FOUND ONE WHO'S FULL GROWN!
YEAH! AND THEN SOME!
!!
GOOD! THEN YOU'LL UNDERSTAND WHY I'M OBLIGED TO STEAL HER!!

WHAT'S THE **MATTER,** STRING? LOST YOUR SENSE OF HUMOR?

YOU BET!

THAT'S IT-- WALK AWAY! **LET ME GO!** WITHOUT ANY TROOPS, YOU CAN'T TAKE PRISONERS, AND THE RULES WON'T LET YOU SHOOT 'EM! OR DO YOU FIGURE I'M ON TO SOMETHING **BIG,** AND THINK I'M DUMB ENOUGH TO LEAD YOU TO IT?
HMMM!!

THAT NIGHT, AFTER BRECKENRIDGE AND HIS MEN HAVE SEARCHED EVERY FOOT OF THE AIRBUS--
THERE'S NO LOOT! NO SLAVES! NOTHING ON THAT BUS, SAM! SO-- **START TALKIN'!** WHAT WAS YOU **AFTER??**
THAT'S **MY** BUSINESS.
NO, SAHIB. **IS OURS!**

WRONG! I'LL TELL YOU WHAT I WANT WHEN I WANT IT! NOW **BACK OFF!!**

KRAK
YEAH! **TALK** TO US!!
NOW **TALK** TO US!

NEXT MORNING, ON THE VERANDA OF THE CHRYSLER RIFLES' RECRUITING DEPOT--
HEY! YOU NEED ME! THIS WOMAN RACKET STUFF HAS TO BE STOPPED!!
FOR THE LAST TIME, YOU'RE NOT JOINING THIS REGIMENT!
OH YES, I AM! YOU'VE GOT NO CHOICE!
I GRADUATED FROM GRANADA COMBAT HIGH AND I'VE MADE THE DOWN PAYMENT ON MY COMMERCIAL COMBAT LICENSE. IT'S ALL IN YOUR COMPUTER. GO ON, LOOK IT UP! YOU'LL SEE!

BESIDES, IF SOMETHING HAPPENS TO THE COLUMN, THERE'S NO ONE TO HELP YOU SAVE THAT GIRL-- EXCEPT ME!

SORRY, KID--IT WON'T WORK. PERSONALLY, I'D LIKE TO HAVE YOU AROUND. YOU'VE GOT GUTS! BUT SERGEANT McCHESNEY WILL NEVER NEVER ALLOW A FEMALE IN THE CHRYSLER RIFLES.

THAT'S NOT A DECISION HE OR ANYONE ELSE CAN MAKE. I KNOW, BECAUSE--

--MY FATHER ONCE COM-MANDED THIS OUTFIT.

NICE TRY, BUT-- HEY! TAKE OFF THAT UNIFORM!!

*TO SEE HOW SPICY SEES HERSELF AS A CADET, SEE COVER.

DAYS LATER, DEEP IN THE HEART OF THE MALAY JUNGLE...
AT LAST! TIE HER IN PLACE!

NO!

NO!
GROAN
PERFECT!

WAIT! DRESS HER IN THE GARMENTS WE BROUGHT FOR THE "AWAITED ONE."

AT THE SAME TIME, FAR TO THE EAST, McCHESNEY'S COLUMN FINDS JANE'S TRAIL AND--
LOOK! UP THERE ON THE CLIFFS!

AMBUSH! EVERY MAN FOR HIMSELF!!

THUD
CRUNCH
SPLAT!

A SINGLE FIGURE RISES FROM THE RUBBLE AND LOOKS UP.
Huh!

MONKEYS!

ALL RIGHT, YOU CURS! YOUR TURN!

RRR

LATER, SEVERAL APES REACH THE ALTAR...
...WITH A GIFT FOR THEIR SAVAGE QUEEN.
WELL DONE! THE PROUD SERGEANT IS INDEED A SPLENDID OFFERING.
AS A REWARD, TELL YOUR MASTER, LORD CHANG, THAT I, NEFFER, HIGH PRIESTESS OF THE LORD GOD MOLOCH'S SACRED FLAME, HAVE...
...A GIFT FOR HIM!
GOOD GAWD!

WITH APOLOGIES TO THE SCULPTURE FRÉMIET.

MEANWHILE, BACK AT THE RECRUITING DEPOT...
I CAN'T BELIEVE WE'RE STILL HERE!
RRRR
DON'T FORGET MY SHIRTS.
I MEAN-- GOSH! WITH THAT POOR GIRL IN SUCH TROUBLE, I'D THINK A REAL CHRYSLER RIFLE WOULD DO SOMETHING, REGARDLESS OF ORDERS!
THE SUGAR BOWL'S EMPTY.
USN
COMIN' UP! YOU KNOW, FROM WHAT MY FATHER TOLD ME ABOUT THAT JUNGLE, THERE'S A GOOD CHANCE THAT COLUMN COULD BE LOST OR SOME-THING!
AND WHO KNOWS WHAT HORRIBLE THINGS THOSE SAVAGES ARE DOING TO HER!

EPISODE
2

THE DEVIL DANCER

WHAT A DUMB CLUB!!!
THE BLUE PARROT, STRING AND SPICY GRAB LUNCH:

LATER, OUTSIDE:
...I MEAN, IT'S DUMB! WATCHING NAKED DANCERS IN A COUNTRY WHERE EVERYONE GOES NAKED! WE SHOULD BE--
KNOCK IT OFF!! WE'RE STAYING HERE!!
BUT WHY? IF SOMETHING'S HAPPENED TO McCHESNEY, YOU'RE IN COMMAND! AND--
--NOTHING'S GOING TO HAPPEN HERE!!!
WHAM!

BRECKENRIDGE'S OLD GANG MEMBERS, NOW LED BY KERSAC, DROP BY THE CLUB ON--

--THEIR WAY TO THE CHRYSLER RIFLES' RECRUITING STATION.

WHEN STRING AND SPICY RECOVER, THEY INSPECT WHAT'S LEFT OF THE STATION:
WOW! WHAT WERE THEY AFTER?

THAT WOULD BE ME, MA'AM. MY BOYS ARE A TAD PISSED, SO I'M OBLIGED TO ASK FOR THE REGIMENT'S PROTECTION.

HERE THEY COME AGAIN!

DRAG HIM INTO THE FLAG ROOM! HURRY!!

I OUGHT TO LET 'EM HAVE HIM--BUT HE'S ON TO SOMETHING! SOMETHING BIG!!

OUTSIDE:
BAM
BAM
BAM

STRING RETREATS TO THE FLAG ROOM:
CLACK
OK!! THAT SHOULD HOLD THEM... FOR ABOUT THREE MINUTES! SO--

--SPILL IT, BRECKENRIDGE! WHAT DO THEY WANT? WHAT ARE YOU UP TO? TALK!
SURE! MY PLEASURE, PARTNER--PROVIDING I GET THE REGIMENT'S PROTECTION! HERE'S MY COMBAT LICENSE. SIGN ME UP!

STRING SLIDES THE LICENSE INTO THE COMPUTER, PRESSES THE ENLISTMENT BUTTON:
OK! YOU'RE IN! NOW START--
HENH

WHAT'S WRONG?
I'M AFRAID, MA'AM, YOUR FRIEND JUST DISCOVERED THE COMPUTER RE-ENLISTED ME AT MY FORMER RANK, TECH-SERGEANT, WHICH, BEING A GRADE HIGHER THAN SERGEANT, MEANS I'M NOW IN COMMAND!

YOU'RE NOT GETTING AWAY WITH THIS, SAM!
DON'D BEDDONIT!
WHAM
I HOPE SHE'S WEARIN' "GRADE A" BODY ARMOR!
SHUT UP AND PUSH!
WHOA! WHAT AM I SEEING?
MORE THAN YOU DESERVE, THAT'S FOR SURE!
HEY! HELP ME! I CAN'T MOVE!!

GRAB HER AND THE GEAR! WE'RE LEAVIN'!!

A HIDDEN STAIRCASE! NOT A BAD OPENER-- NOW WHAT?
JUST MOVE IT, SERGEANT! FAST!

AS THEY GO DEEPER AND DEEPER, SPICY RECOVERS.
SO WHERE'D YOU GET THE SWELL OUTFIT?
MY DAD! IT'S A REAL OLD MODEL. THAT'S WHY IT ACTS UP SOMETIMES. THE LAB GUYS SAID IT'S JUST MY BODY CHEMISTRY. DAD--
--TOLD ME... MY MOM MADE IT.
THAT FIGURES. THE LOCAL LADIES DO LOVE THEIR HOCUS-POCUS.
A NATIVE MOTHER! Ahhhh!
THEY REACH A SUB-TERRANEAN TUNNEL.
OH, WOW!
EXACTLY! A GENUINE B-52 CHESTERFIELD HIDDEN BY ONE SHREWD TECH SERGEANT. SPICY, YOU TAKE THE RUMBLE SEAT. STRING, YOU DRIVE!
WHERE WE HEADED?
YOU'LL SEE!

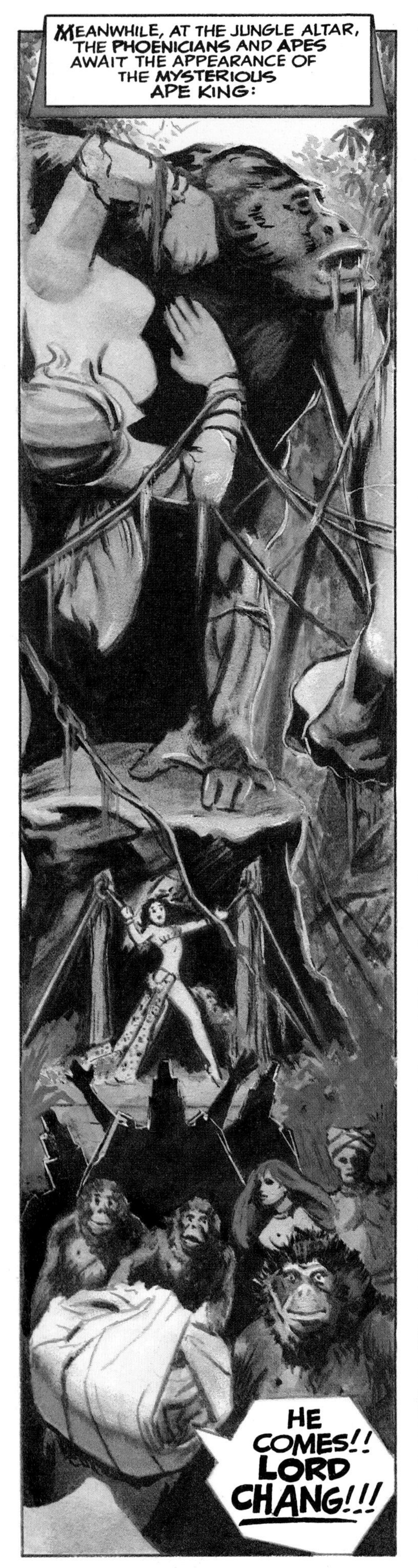
MEANWHILE, AT THE JUNGLE ALTAR, THE PHOENICIANS AND APES AWAIT THE APPEARANCE OF THE MYSTERIOUS APE KING:
HE COMES!! LORD CHANG!!!

RRRRR
UP THERE!!

RRR
Ahhhh! IT SOUNDS LIKE THIS ONE PLEASES HIM.
NOW WE'LL DEAL WITH BRECKENRIDGE AND THE "AWAITED ONE"!! JAKTAR!!
DUM DUM DUM DUM

BY THE DAWN AND NIGHTS OF TEN--
DUM DUM DUM
--BY THE EVEN AND THE ODD--
--LET THE DEVIL DANCE--

--WITH FIRE AND PAIN--
--THE TIGER'S STRIPES--
--THE WIND'S BREATH,
--DELIVER THEM TO MOLOCH!!!

SIMULTANEOUSLY, AT THE AIRBUS CRASH SITE OUTSIDE PORT MACAO:
ALL RIGHT, SAM, WHAT ARE WE LOOKING FOR?
A MAP-- WHICH I FIGURE IS HIDING IN SAUNDERS' TRUNK!
I THINK I SEE IT!

A MAP!!
A TREASURE MAP! NEFFER WANTS IT REAL BAD, SO I LED HER TO THE WRONG TRAIL AND SHE STOLE YOUR GIRL INSTEAD OF--

--OUR LITTLE BLONDE FRIEND. NOW THE NEXT MOVE IS HERS.

Uh-oh!

THAT'S RIGHT, SAUNDERS, I KNOW ALL ABOUT IT!
ALL ABOUT WHAT? THERE'S NO TREASURE, JUST A RIVER! HONEST!! MY DAD SAID IF I BATHED IN IT, I'D BE--
THAT'S THE ONE! HAND IT OVER!!

BUT IT'S PERSONAL. I PROMISED DAD I--
WHEN WE FIND IT, YOU CAN BATHE ALLLLL YOU WANT. NOW BE A GOOD SOLDIER AND--
OKAY! OKAY! BUT I NEED SOME TIME TO PREPARE IT.

NIGHTTIME:
KEEP YOUR BACKS TURNED!
ALL RIGHT! ALL RIGHT!
WHAT A BORE!

YOU'RE TAKING ALL NIGHT!

OKAY-- NOW!

AWK!

MY GAWDD!!
WHOA! OUR APOLOGIES, MA'AM! WE HAD NO IDEA WHAT WE WERE ASKING!!
Hmm! YOU DON'T LOOK SO BORED NOW, STRING! SAM, IF YOU WANNA READ IT, COME OVER HERE IN THE FIRELIGHT. IT'S KINDA FADED.
MY PLEASURE, MA'AM! I'M ON MY WAY.
WATCH OUT FOR THESE CRAZY PARROTS!
Ah, YES, LOVELY. MORE OF MOMMY'S WORK?
Uh huh. THE FLAME INDICATES THE "RIVER OF THE ARROW." IT RUNS UNDER THE TEMPLE OF MOLOCH. THE--
--DIRECTIONS FROM PORT MACAO ARE ON MY BACK.
INDEED THEY ARE! WELL, STRING, THE LEGENDARY TREASURE RIVER AND THE TEMPLE OF MOLOCH WHERE THEY'LL BE HOLDING YOUR GIRL!! IS THAT BIG ENOUGH FOR YOU?
Oh, YEAH! BUT I'M NOT GETTING ANOTHER WOMAN IN THIS MESS! SPICY STAYS IN PORT MACAO!!
WAIT A SEC! IT'S M--
RIGHT! SHE'D ONLY SLOW US DOWN. SO I'LL GET A PENCIL AND "YOU" CAN COPY THE MAP.

MORNING, ABOVE PORT MACAO:
BUT IT'S MY MAP!!! THIS ISN'T FAIR!
THAT'S RIGHT! BUT IT'S DONE!
NOT QUITE! THAT'S MY GANG IN THAT TIGER SHIP!

THEIR LIFTERS HAVEN'T GOT IT! GET ABOVE 'EM!
HEY! CUT THAT OUT!
YEAH! GET ABOVE 'EM!

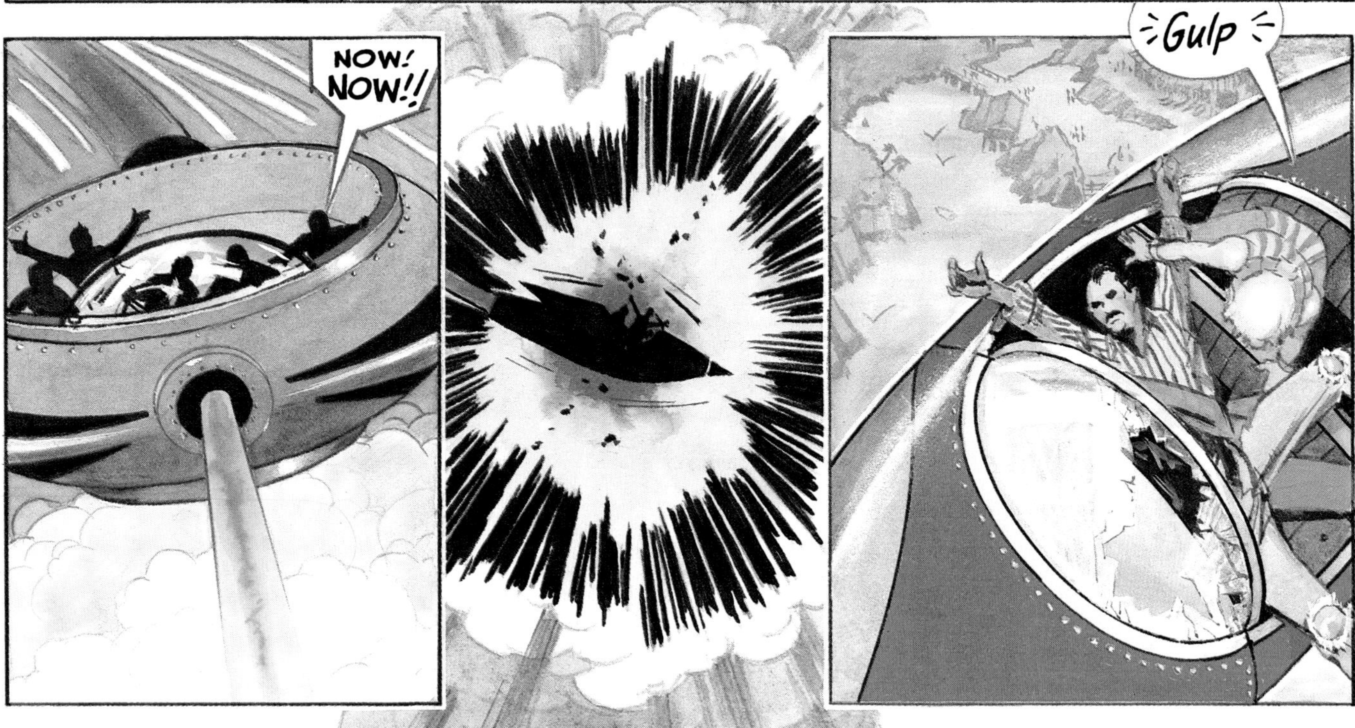
NOW! NOW!!
Gulp

SPICY SHOVES STRING AND SAM ASIDE AND TAKES CONTROL.
OK! LET'S SHOW THESE BUMS OUR DUST!
PUT PUT

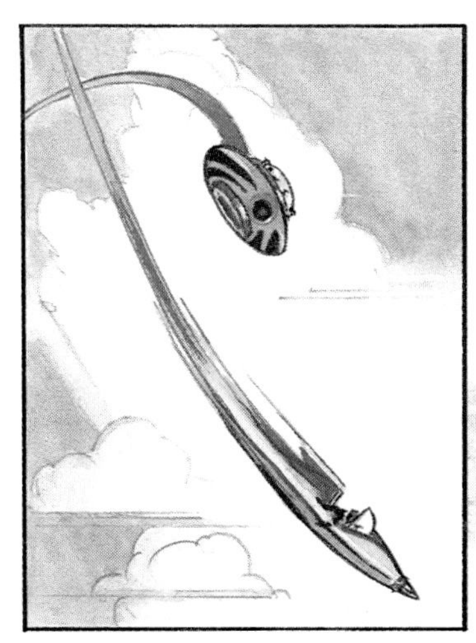

WOW!!! NOW WE'RE TALKIN'!!

YOW! THAT HURTS!

CAN'T OUT-RUN 'EM, SO--

WHUMP

HOURS LATER:
HEY! WHAT HAPPENED?
WHERE ARE WE?

ON OUR WAY TO THE RIVER OF THE ARROW!

DAWN--SOMEWHERE DEEP IN THE MALAY JUNGLE, JANE AWAKES:
UNHHHH A CAVE?
COME! MUST DRESS!!
ULP YOU TALK!
SURE! TALK GOOD!
OKAY! BUT, GOSH! I CAN DO THAT!
MOVE NO!
JANE IS LED TO--
--CHANG'S LAIR:
WHAT!! THIS CAN'T BE!
THAT'S ME!!!
YES. YOU SA-FRA-FISCO.
RIGHT! AT THE PRESIDENT'S FOLLIES! BUT HOW--
QUIET! HE HERE!
ULP

CHANG, APE KING OF THE ALAR, GUARDIANS OF THE FORBIDDEN WAY.
H... H... H... HI!
YOU 'FRAID?
Y... Y... YES, SIR. Um... MY PICTURE... UP THERE...
...DOES THAT, I MEAN, YOU KNOW, uh...
IT OK. YOU SEE BETTER ONE TONIGHT... WHERE I SLEEP.
SLEEP!!!
Gasp

MEANWHILE, SAM, STRING, AND SPICY CLIMB AN OUTCROPPING OVERLOOKING THE MALAY HEARTLAND:
WE'RE ON COURSE! THERE ARE THE BREASTS OF TANIT! THE PASS WE WANT RUNS BETWEEN THEM.
IT'LL TAKE US A WEEK THROUGH THAT JUNGLE!
NOT IF WE FLY OVER IT!
BACK ON THE JUNGLE FLOOR . . .
FORGET IT, SAM. THE CANOPY'S OVER TEN STORIES HIGH. THIS CRATE'S LIFTERS CAN'T HOLD THAT KIND OF ALTITUDE.
DON'T BRING ME PROBLEMS, SERGEANT! BRING ME ANSWERS!
YOU'RE BLOWING IT, SAM!
JUST WATCH AND LEARN, KID!
Whoops!
WE'RE DROPPING!!!
KRAASH
GOT IT!
CRACK
THAT DOES IT, SAM! YOU'RE A DEAD MAN!

YOW!

SAM!! STRING!!
YEEOOOWW!!!!
DAMN IT, STRING! Puf-Puf IF YOU'RE SURE OF SOMETHING-- GROAN HAVE THE GUTS TO TALK ME INTO IT!
SAM-- Gasp SHUT UP!
LATER--AFTER SPICY HAS RETRIEVED THEIR SCATTERED GEAR:
WE GOTTA KEEP MOVING, SO I'LL CARRY YOUR STUFF UNTIL YOU GET YOUR WIND. AND YOU BETTER BUTTON UP, NIGHT'S COMING ON. READY?
BOY! WAS DAD RIGHT! THIS IS THE LIFE!!!

NIGHT--CHANG'S SLEEPING QUARTERS:
THAT'S ME, ALL RIGHT -- WHEN I PLAYED THE ORPHEUM CIRCUIT.

I ALWAYS THOUGHT IT WAS TOO CHI-CHI! WHAT DO YOU THINK?
NO LIKE IN FUR. TAKE OFF!

AW, NO! NOT YOU, TOO!!

OBEY!!

OKAY! SURE! I KNOW THIS BIT!! (Oh, BOY! I GOTTA GET OUTTA HERE!)
LOOK IN BOX! WAIT HERE!
Gee! HE DIDN'T EVEN LOOK AT ME! THE BRUTE!!

Hmmm! SO THIS IS WHAT HE LIKES!
MAYBE I "CAN" HANDLE HIM!!

ARRRR
RRRRRR

LATER
PLEASE... PLEASE DON'T HURT ME!
OOHHH!!

WEEKS LATER...
THAT'S IT! THE FOR-BIDDEN WAY!
FORBIDDEN! THAT MEANS GUARDS!
RIGHT! WE GOTTA MOVE FAST!
THEY DROP THEIR EXCESS GEAR AND:
STAY IN THE SHADOWS!
WE ARE, DAMMIT! HURRY UP!
GOOD GAWD!
McCHESNEY'S COLUMN!
WHAT'S LEFT OF IT!
NOTHING WE CAN DO HERE. LET'S MOVE!
THE END OF THE PASS:
IT SHOULD BE RIGHT--
--THERE!
Whoa! THAT'S GNARLY!

NO RIVER! NO SAVAGES! NOTHING !!
YES, SIR!
DON'T COUNT ON IT! SPICY, GIVE ME THAT RIFLE AND GET TO THE REAR!
AAAAGG!!
HEY! THAT'S A WOMAN'S SCREAM!
SPICY, DON'T!!
SPICY! WAIT!
STAIRS SHAKING! Oh, GREAT! A DRAWBRIDGE!
SCREEE RRR

EMPTY! NO! THE AIR SHAFT ON THE FLOOR!
AAAGGG!!!

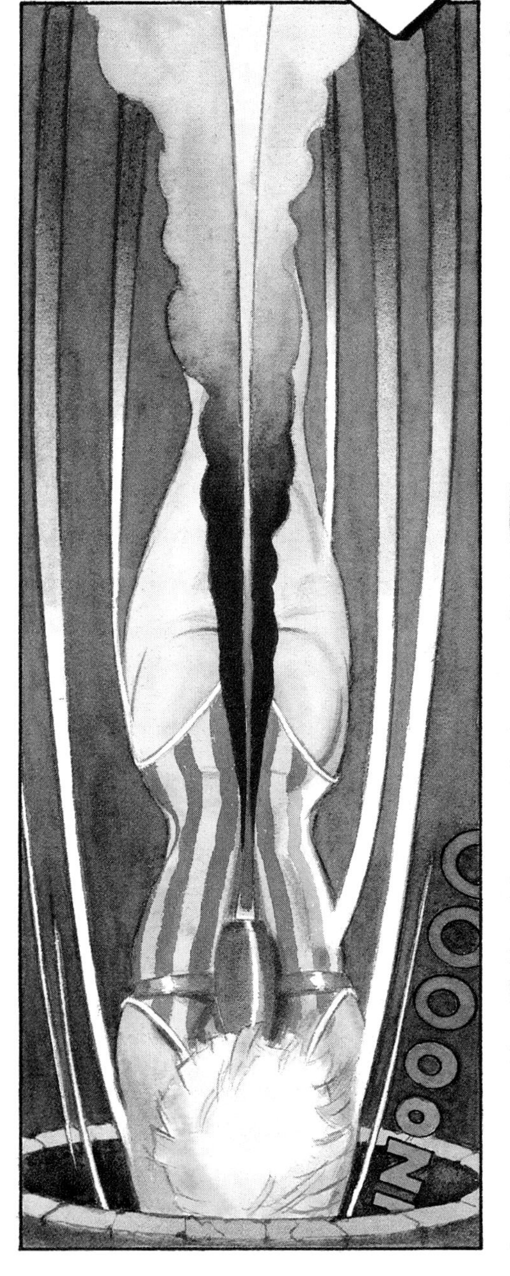
NOOOOO

ANOTHER SIDE SHAFT! BUT THE SCREAM IS STILL FURTHER DOWN!
AAGG!

CLANG
WE'RE TRAPPED!
BRILLIANT, STRING! JUST BRILLIANT! THERE'S HER VAPOR TRAIL! MOVE IT!

FAR BELOW, SPICY EMERGES FROM AN AIR SHAFT:
HOLY SMOKE!

MOM!
SPICY MOVES IN FOR A CLOSER LOOK AND:
YIPE!

BACK IN THE MAIN TEMPLE:
THAT'S SPICY'S VOICE!
I KNOW! HANG ON!
IKE!
KRACK
Ahhh! THE LIAR IS OURS!
NOW, SEAL THE SHAFT!
OOOF
HEY! DON'T--
THUD
NUTS!!
STRING CRAWLS DEEPER AND DEEPER THROUGH A LABYRINTH OF AIR SHAFTS, THEN:
FINALLY! SOME LIGHT!!
WELL DONE! NOW SEND WORD TO THE TRIBES THAT MOLOCH IS READY TO RECIEVE THIER OFFERINGS AND LIGHT THE FIRES!

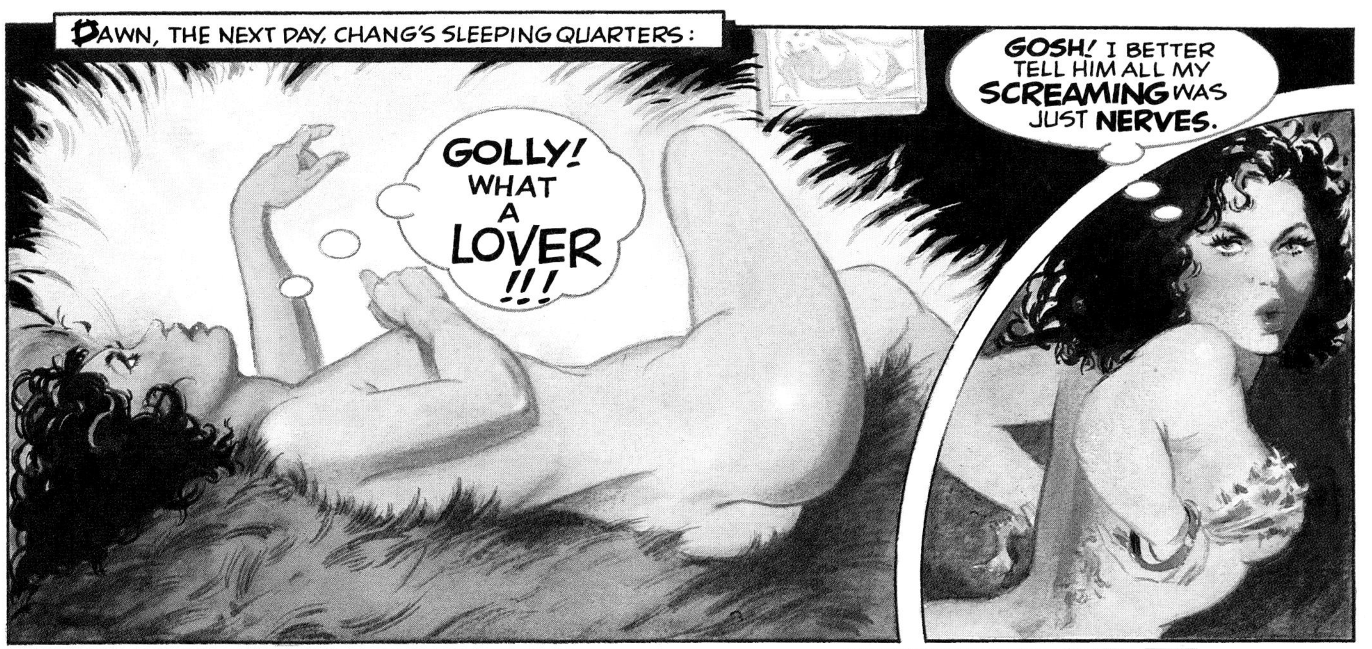
DAWN, THE NEXT DAY, CHANG'S SLEEPING QUARTERS:
GOLLY! WHAT A LOVER!!!
GOSH! I BETTER TELL HIM ALL MY SCREAMING WAS JUST NERVES.

MOMENTS LATER:
HI, GUYS, HAVE YOU SEEN--
TAKE HER!!!

INSTANTLY, JANE IS SUBDUED AND CARRIED OFF:
Oh, GAWD, NO! NOW HE DOESN'T RESPECT ME!

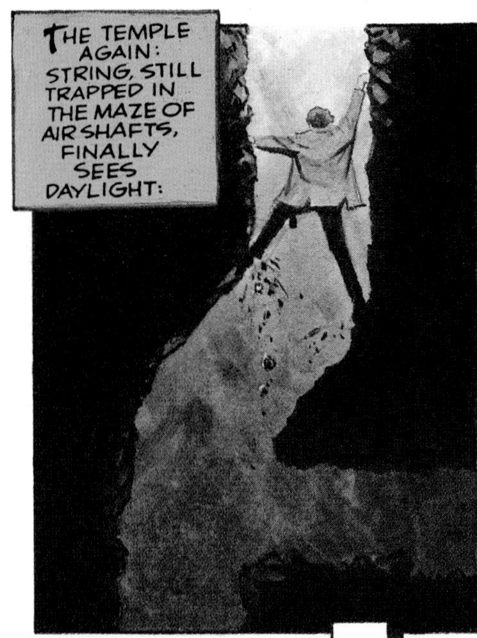
THE TEMPLE AGAIN: STRING, STILL TRAPPED IN THE MAZE OF AIR SHAFTS, FINALLY SEES DAYLIGHT:

Ah hah! A WAY OUT!

GOOD LORD!

THE JUNGLE'S GONE MAD!!

HEY! THAT LOOKS LIKE LI--
JANE!!

EPISODE 3

BOUND AND GAGGED

IT'S USELESS TO FIGHT ME, SMALL ONE. CAUSING YOUR GARMENT TO VANISH WILL NOT KEEP ME FROM STEALING IT. AND--
INSIDE THE TEMPLE, SPICY IS DRAGGED TO NEFFER'S QUARTERS.
--AS IT FADES, IT WILL REVEAL THE MAP DRAWN ON YOUR FLESH TO TELL ME YOU ARE INDEED THE--
--"AWAITED ONE!"
THIS IS SO, MASTER, BUT THIS MAP SHOWS A RIVER BENEATH THE TEMPLE, AND THERE IS NO RIVER!
THERE IS FOR THOSE WHO CAN SEE IT. NOW GO! TELL THE TEMPLE PRIESTS--

MOMENTS LATER:
DUM DUM DUM
--TO BEGIN THE CEREMONY.
HEAR THAT? THE DRUMS ANNOUNCE MOLOCH'S PLEASURE AT YOUR ARRIVAL. YOUR FATHER COULD HAVE--
--EXPLAINED WHY, BUT YOUR MOTHER, NO DOUBT, FORBID IT. YOU SEE, SHE WAS MOLOCH'S RIVAL! THE FOUL ASHERAT! AND YOU, IF YOU HAD FOUND THE RIVER, WOULD HAVE TAKEN HER PLACE.
MY Pleasure!
BUT THAT WILL NEVER HAPPEN. AFTER YOU GIVE ME YOUR GARMENT, I WILL GIVE "YOU" TO MOLOCH--JUST AS I GAVE YOUR MOTHER. IT IS MY DUTY!

AT THE SAME MOMENT, OUTSIDE, STRING STRUGGLES ACROSS THE FACE OF THE TEMPLE:
GOTTA GET BACK IN THERE!
WHOOPS!
ARRGG!
ANOTHER GROAN AIR SHAFT!
STRING TUMBLES DOWN A SERIES OF SHAFTS TO THE DUNGEON LEVEL AND:
THUD
OK, STRING! STOP FOOLIN' AROUND!

DUM DUM DUM DUM DUM
EMPTY!
GOTTA FIND WHERE THOSE DRUMS ARE COMING FROM!
DUM DUM
AT THE DOOR TO NEFFER'S QUARTERS:
Hmm! NO DRUMS BUT--
--THIS MIGHT COME IN HANDY!
THEN, AT THE ALTAR DOOR:
DON'T TURN AROUND, BUDDY-- GOTTA GET IN THERE.
DUM DUM
DUM
MAYBE?
YEP! THE FUN'S DEAD AHEAD!
AAGGGGGGGGGHHHHHH
NOOOOO
PLEASE
HELP! HELP! HELP
EYAAAEE

ULP
MOLOCH
MOLOCH
MOLOCH
MOLOCH

AHH, FINALLY WE MEET AGAIN.
BEAUTIFUL, YOU'RE GONNA BE A TOUGH ACT TO FOLLOW.
Hmmm!

UH OH! SOMETHING'S UP AND THERE'S JANE!
SILENCE!

LORD CHANG, MOLOCH HONORS YOU! YOURS WILL BE--

--THE FIRST OFFERING!

MOLOCH MOLOCH
STRING PUNCHES THE FLYING BELT'S IGNITION BUTTON:
AAAGG! IT WON'T START!

GROAN
IT'S ON WRONG!
MOLOCH
MOLOCH
HANG ON. I'M-- OOPS!
Oh, STRING! STRING!! WHERE ARE YOU?
ON MY WAY, ANGEL!
FWOOSH

BRAP
EYAAAH
Oh, STRING! HELP ME!

THERE! UP THERE!
YOW!

OKAY, FOLKS! SHOW-TIME!
WOOSH
THAT'S IT! PANIC!
HENH I'M OUTTA GROAN GAS!
PUT PUT

WELL DONE, SERGEANT. YOU ARE INDEED AMUSING. SO NOW I WILL AMUSE YOU--BY ALLOWING YOUR DANCING GIRL TO LIVE--

--WITH LORD CHANG!

YOU'RE UNREAL!
NO. I SIMPLY UNDERSTAND "THE WAY OF THINGS AS THEY ARE"! MOLOCH'S WAY!
IN THE GIRL'S PLACE, THE SACRED FLAME WILL RECEIVE YOUR REGIMENT'S TOTEMS, YOUR COMRADES, AND YOU!
DON'T COUNT ON IT!
YOUR OPTIMISM IS ADMIRABLE, BUT USELESS. IF THE "AWAITED ONE" HAD LED YOU TO THE RIVER, PERHAPS YOU COULD HAVE LEARNED TO PLAY THE GREAT GAME HER WAY. BUT NOW YOU MUST PLAY IT MY WAY!
BRING HER!

WELCOME, SMALL ONE. ARE YOU PREPARED TO GIVE ME WHAT I WANT?
NEVER
I THOUGHT AS MUCH. MAKE THE KNOT TIGHT!
WHAT'S THE WITCH AFTER?
I'D SAY--
--HER BODY ARMOR!
BODY ARMOR! SHE'S NEEKID!
MAYBE!
MAYBE NOT!

WHACK

WHACK

SHE CAN'T BREAK SPICY!
Hmmph SHE'LL MURDER THE WEE THING, SHE WILL!
SHE'LL TRY, THAT'S SURE!

Oh, PLEASE! MAKE IT ALL STOP!
WHACK

WHACK

WHACK
NEFFER STRIKES AGAIN AND:
Ahhh!
HEY! WHERE'D HER CLOTHES COME FROM?
UH-OH! THERE IT IS!
WELL DONE, SMALL ONE! NOW YOU'LL REMOVE IT OR HAVE IT CUT OFF!
THE CROWD SURGES FORWARD EXCITEDLY. SUDDENLY THERE'S A BLINDING FLASH, THEN--
--SPICY'S BODY ARMOR RADIATES BEAMS OF LIGHT OVER THEIR STARTLED FACES AND--

--EVERYONE GOES JOYOUSLY NUTS!
CHESSUS! NOW WHAT?
IT'S HER BODY ARMOR! IT MAKES YOU SEE THINGS--NOT AS THEY ARE--BUT AS YOU WISH THEY WERE. SHE'S A PLAYER, ALL RIGHT!
CUT IT OUT, SAM! WHAT'S--
GO AHEAD! YOU'RE FULL GROWN. SEE FOR YOURSELF!
EYAHH!

SAM! YOU SEE WHAT I SEE?
NOT LIKELY.

THAT'S ENOUGH OF THAT!
WHACK
IT IS TRUTH! MY DREAM HAPPENS! THE PICTURE ON MY WALL--

--COMES ALIVE!

NEFFER ADVANCES TO STRIKE AGAIN AND:
STOP HIM!
THWACK
ANGERED BY THE ATTACK ON THEIR KING, THE APES CHARGE.

GRAB HIS KEYS!
KRAK
GOT 'EM!
SIMULTANEOUSLY, BEDLAM ERUPTS AND MOLOCH LOSES HIS TEMPER.
KABOOM

AT THE FOOT OF THE ALTAR:

THE SAME INSTANT, A FEW FEET AWAY:
THE GUNS, STRING! THE GUNS!
HANG ON! I CAN'T SEE A THING!

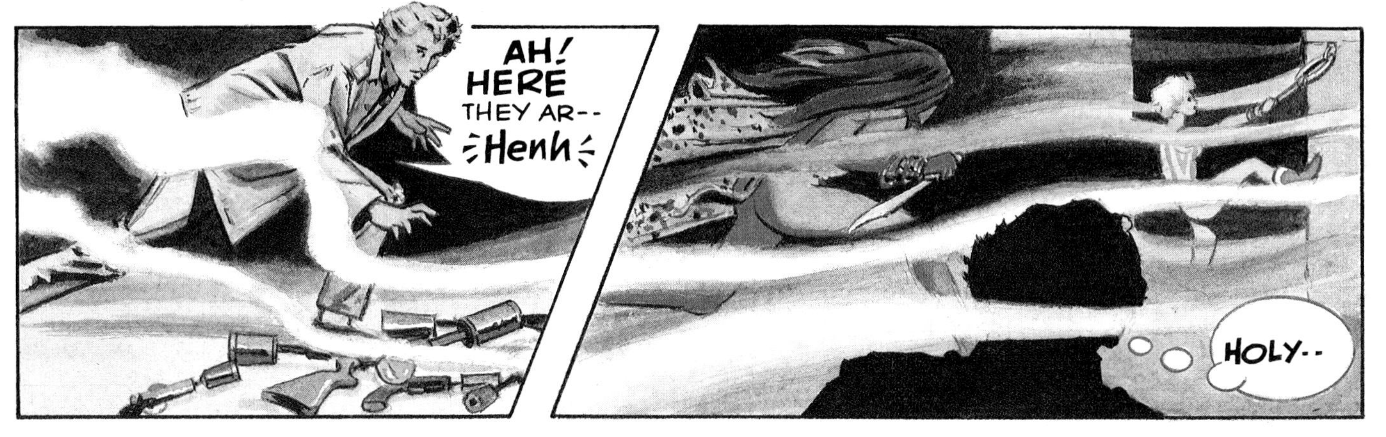
AH! HERE THEY AR--
Henh
HOLY..

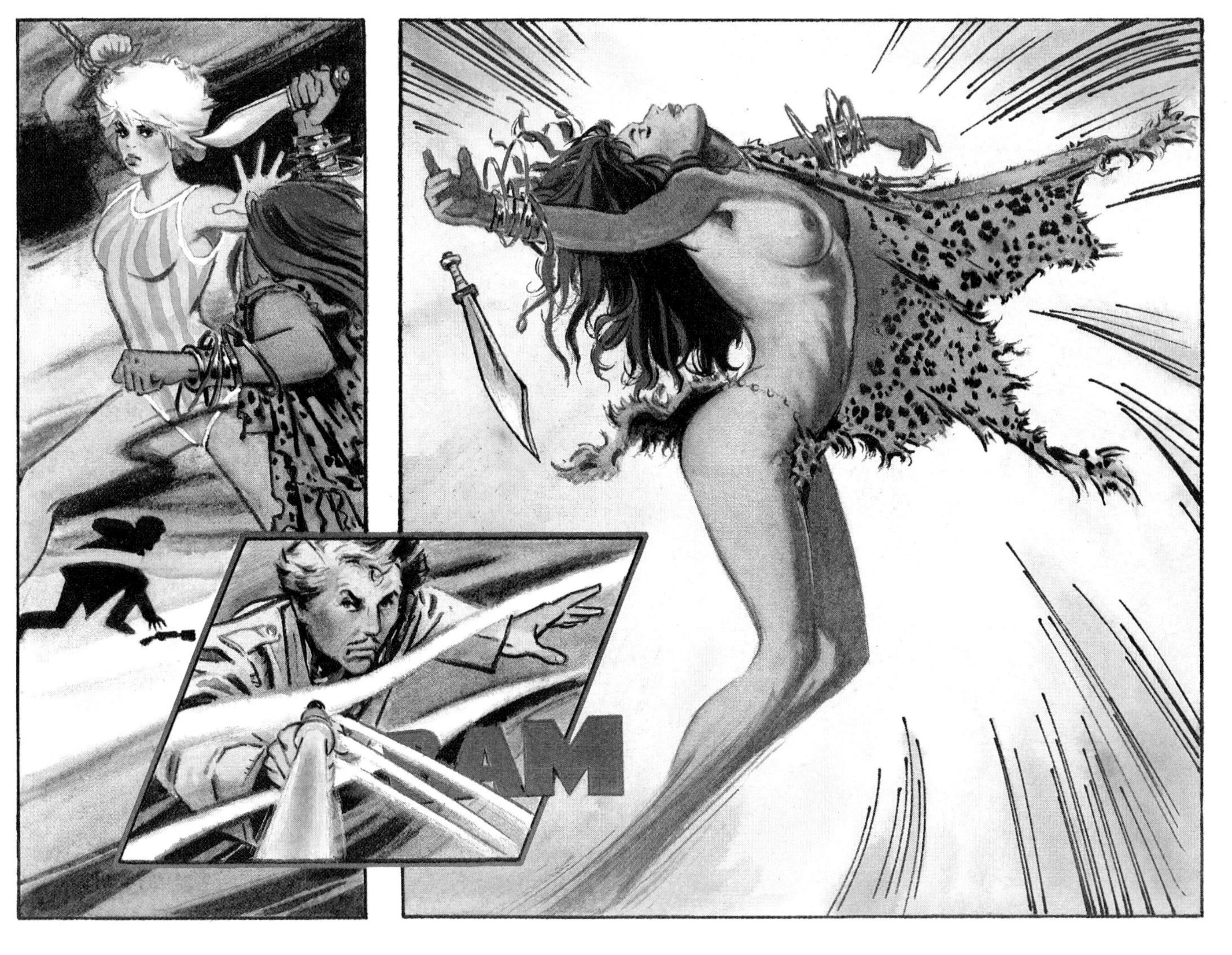

THERE! NOW LET'S DITCH THIS HELLHOLE!

THE CAPTIVE WOMEN FLEE TO THE SOLDIERS.
HEAD FOR THE DOOR! FOLLOW US!

HERE! MOVE IT!

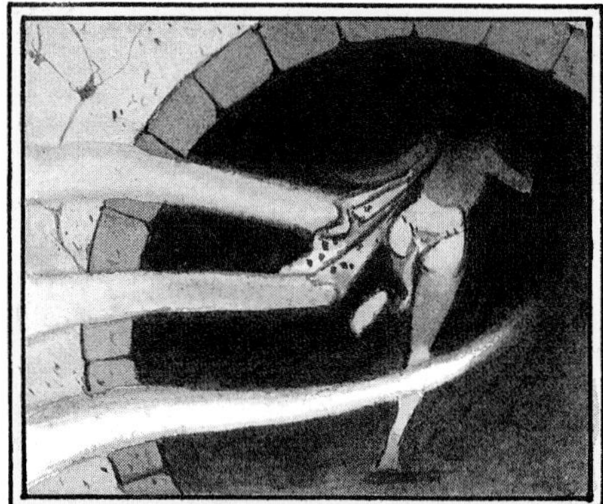

SHE'S GETTING AWAY!
LET HER!

I CAN'T!

MOMENTS LATER, DEEP IN THE TEMPLE DUNGEONS:
HOLD IT RIGHT THERE!

THUD
CLACK
BLAM
SPICY CLIMBS THROUGH THE SPLINTERED DOOR.
NOW!
WHERE'S THE RIVER?

YOU DON'T **REALLY** THINK I'LL **TELL** YOU?
SPLATT
A LOT MORE OF THE SAME, THEN:
NOW *Sigh* **SPILL** IT!
ALL RIGHT! *Moan* ALL **RIGHT**.
RED HAR-VEST

THE RIVER FLOWS RIGHT WHERE YOU STAND. THROUGH YOUR FATHER'S LIBRARY!
MY FATHER'S WHAT? QUIT STALLING!
YOU DOUBT ME? LOOK!
WHAT TH--!!!
HOW'D YOU DO THAT?
VARSITY OF THE CLIFFHANGERS
LOVE STORY
DOES IT MATTER? NOW YOU CAN BATHE IN IT! WASH YOURSELF FREE OF THE "WHEEL OF THINGS AS THEY ARE." FREE OF MOLOCH!
SUDDENLY:
HENH IT'S GONE! IT WAS JUST--
--AN ILLUSION. YES! YOU WANTED TO SEE IT SO BADLY, YOU DID. BUT YOU NEVER ACTUALLY WILL. BECAUSE THAT'S ALL IT IS, AN ILLUSION!

BALONEY! IF THIS REALLY IS DAD'S LIBRARY, THEN ONE OF THESE BOOKS WILL SHOW ME THE WAY!
IT'S YOUR FATHER'S ALL RIGHT. GO AHEAD!
READ THEM! READ THEM ALL! BUT THERE'S NOTHING HERE BUT A LOT OF WORTHLESS OLD JUNK HE DUG OUT OF THE JUNGLE!
BEDTIME Stories
GLASS KEY
SO WHAT! DAD LOVED TRASH! I'LL BET--
HEY! THE THREE MUSKETEERS! WOW!
NEFFER PRESSES A HIDDEN BUTTON AND:
WOOSH
SHE'S GONE! I GROAN BLEW IT!
THUMP
SUDDENLY:
YIPE!

ANOTHER QUAKE LIKE THAT AND THE WHOLE THING WILL CAVE IN!
MEANWHILE, OUTSIDE, EVERYONE HAS FLED EXCEPT THE SOLDIERS AND RESCUED WOMEN.
IF YOU'RE THINKIN' ABOUT GOIN' BACK IN THERE TO RESCUE THAT WEE CADET, FORGET IT! SHE BRUNG IT ON HERSELF, SHE DID. BESIDES, WE GOT WHAT WE CAME FOR!
RELAX, STRING! THAT APE-MAN WILL LOOK AFTER HER!
YEAH! RIGHT! WE SURE TOOK CARE OF JANE, ALL RIGHT!
HE'S RIGHT, STRING!
I'LL BE FINE, HONEST. YOU WERE JUST SUPER, BUT, WELL, YOU KNOW ME. I CAN'T HELP MYSELF, AND CHANG IS SO OPEN. SO SINCERE! I DIDN'T KNOW IT COULD BE LIKE THAT. AND WHATEVER HAPPENED IN THERE BROKE NEFFER'S SPELL OVER HIM. NOW I'M SURE HE'LL BEHAVE.
BEHAVE! HE'S AN ANIMAL!
I KNOW! I KNOW! I THINK THAT'S WHAT I LIKE BEST!

SORE LOSER, HUH!

YOU BET!

SIMULTANEOUSLY:
HEY! GREAT PUNCH!
WASN'T ME. ANOTHER QUAKE!

SPICY'S HAD IT.
Oh? LOOK AGAIN!

HEY! IT'S ME!!
WHOA!

I HAD HER, SAM, BUT SHE--uh--GOT AWAY.
WHAT'S THIS? TREASURE?
FIGURES. AND THE RIVER? THE TREASURE?

GREAT! NOW WE'RE COOKIN'.
WELL, IT TURNED OUT THAT MY MAP LED TO MY FATHER'S LIBRARY. SO I FIGURED ONE OF HIS BOOKS WOULD SHOW US THE WAY AND GRABBED A BUNCH.

THAT'LL BE ENOUGH OF THAT, CADET! I'M IN COMMAND OF THIS OUTFIT AND YOU REPORT TO ME, SERGEANT McCHESNEY! SO I'LL BE TAKIN' THOSE BOOKS!

YES, SIR, SERGEANT McCHESNEY SIR!
NOW GIT A UNIFORM OFF THE WAGON--AND STAY OUT OF ME SIGHT.
AS FER YOU RENEGADES! START FIGURIN' OUT HOW THE TWO OF YA ARE GONNA RECRUIT A WHOLE NEW REGIMENT! NOW MOUNT UP!

!!!
#@%!!
RELAX, BRECKENRIDGE, HOW HARD CAN IT BE TO STEAL A FEW BOOKS?

WEEKS LATER, THEY SIGHT PORT MACAO.
THEN AGAIN, MAYBE THAT MAP DRAWN ON HER IS A SYMBOL? A METAPHOR--SAYING SPICY'S THE ONE WHO'LL LEAD US TO THE TREASURE! THAT'S IT, SAM. TRUST YOUR INSTINCTS-- STICK WITH THE GIRL!
BOY! I COULD SURE USE A BURGER AND SOME FRIES!
IT'S OBVIOUS, STRING. IF HER BODY ARMOR CAN PUT ON A SHOW LIKE IT DID IN THAT TEMPLE-- THEN WHY NOT A SHOW WITH A FEW BUBBLE BEADS AND A G-STRING?
Hmmm!
THE END?

PREVIEWS
OF COMING EPISODES!!!
STRING HIRES A NEW DANCER! SIX OR SEVEN NEW DANCERS! A WHOLE CHORUS LINE!
TABAKKA
McCHESNEY VOWS TO FIND THE RIVER OF THE ARROW-AND USE ITS TREASURE TO REBUILD THE REGIMENT.
SPICY IS USED FOR TARGET PRACTICE!!
"STRING" GOES TO HIS LEFT!!

Silke '95
NEFFER IS CIVILIZED BY JOEL ORCHID

A MYSTERIOUS BANDIT TRIBE RESCUES OUR HEROES.
WHO IS SHE? WHAT'S SHE WANT? AND "WHO" WANTS HER?
SOJIN-MAGICIAN? MADMAN! PATRIOT!
McCHESNEY TAKES THINGS INTO HIS OWN HANDS!
DIRT FORT - ANCIENT HOME OF THE CHRYSLER RIFLES - GUARDS THE PASS TO THE "VALLEY OF JUNK."

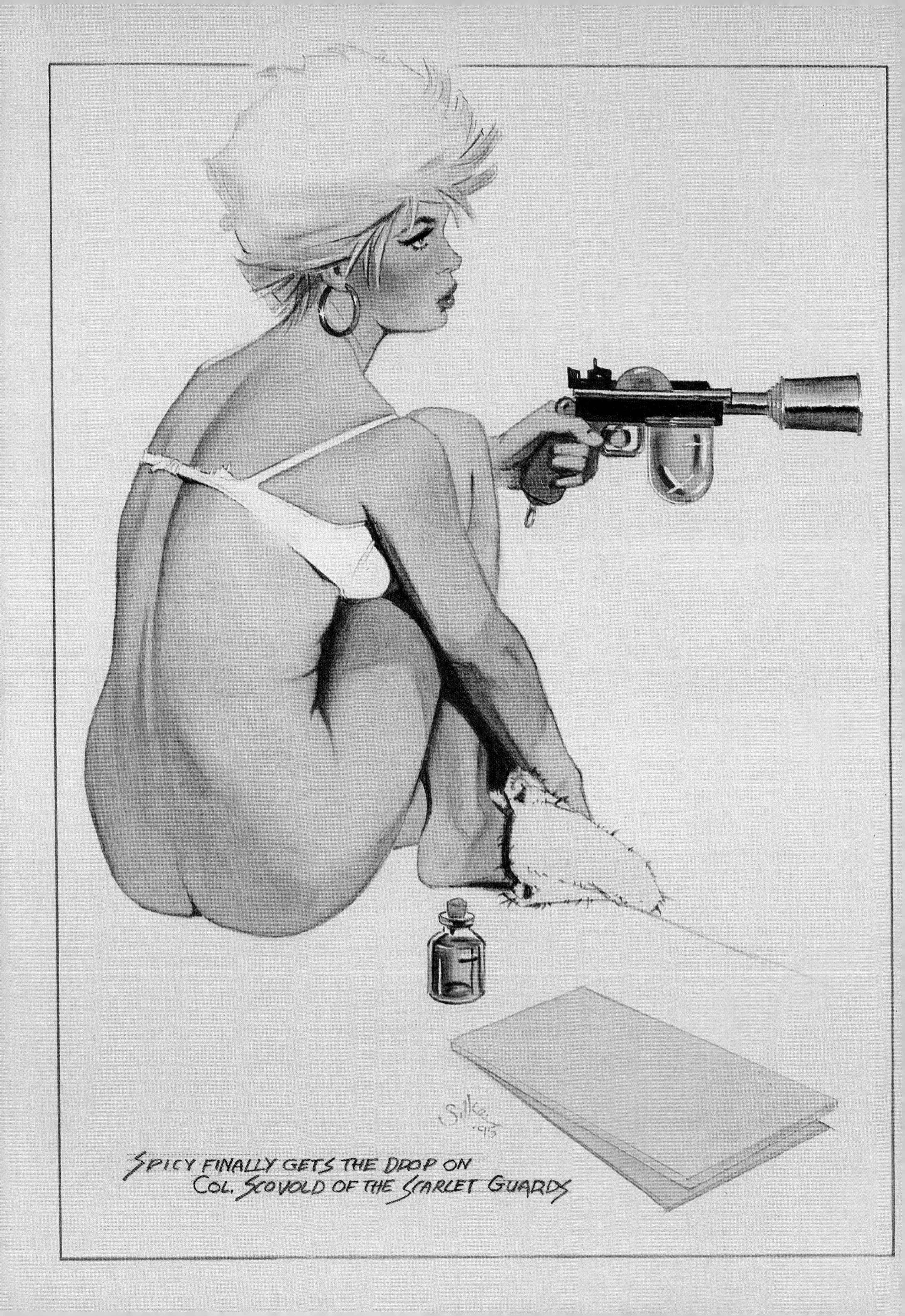
Silke '95
SPICY FINALLY GETS THE DROP ON
COL. SCOVOLD OF THE SCARLET GUARDS

JANE RETURNS TO DANCING - AND RISKS HER LIFE DOING IT!

SEE YOU IN EPISODE 4

"My Trouble is Dames"

Or "The Slow Birth of RASCALS IN PARADISE"

In January 1961, *Argosy* published an article by Milton Caniff, the creator of "Terry and the Pirates" and "Steve Canyon," titled "My Trouble is Dames." Artist/author Jim Silke recalls, "After reading it, I realized that somehow, someday, I had to draw a comic filled with beautiful, dangerous women. The trouble Caniff referred to, of course, was the Dragon Lady, Miss Lace, Burma, and Cheeta. But my trouble was, I couldn't draw women worth a lick.

"I mean I was *bad*. In an early life-drawing class, after drawing a particularly nubile naked lady, I became embarrassed on realizing I had given all my energy and interest to her breasts and timidly asked the instructor if I had made them too large. He studied my drawing awhile, then politely asked me where her breasts were.

Diane Webber

"Getting the women halfway right is one reason why it's taken me sixty-three years to come up with *Rascals*."

Silke's fascination with comics began in the early thirties with "Buck Rogers" in the Sunday funnies and became an addiction with the arrival of the Golden Age of comic books in the late thirties. "All the kids on my block drew their own comics back then, and most of us copied the same artist, Caniff," says Silke. "I'm sure that my preference for a team of heroes, for the lure of the exotic Orient, and for the comics medium itself were all decisions made for me by Caniff's genius. And, after all, his women were the first women I met who, as he put it, had 'trouble keeping their clothes on.'"

The movies were also a major influence. "For me, the neon signs themselves, of the Roxie, the T&D, the Grand Lake, and the Fox Oakland, were irresistible temptations because, when the movie started, you were instantly thrust into a world populated by goddesses. I had no idea that art directors like Anton Grot, Hans Drier, and Mario Larrinaga had designed those worlds, or that the actresses had

Actress/model Sandy Warner

been clothed by the likes of Milo Anderson, Travis Banton, and Irene. It all simply came with the twenty-five-cent ticket price."

It would be years before Silke recognized the aesthetic those cinematic artists employed and began to study how the exterior beauty of an actress had the potential of serving as a mask for a more profound and affecting inner beauty. Nevertheless, *Rascals* was beginning to take shape.

Silke decided on an art career in 1951 when he dropped out of the University of Redlands and attended Art Center School in Hollywood. Jepson Art Institute was next. When it closed, he followed its fabled drawing instructor, Herb Jepson, "all over L.A." After two years in the army, he worked at several advertising agencies, then, in early 1957, he landed at Capitol Records as assistant art director.

The timing was perfect: in the fifties, the record industry, like the paperback industry, put a beautiful

photo/Silke

woman on almost every cover. The art directors hired the models, directed the photo sessions, and designed the covers. But it wasn't easy. Every guy thinks he knows what a beautiful woman is, but professionally speaking, he doesn't. And he knows even less about dealing with them. "The first model I hired was an actress, named Sandy Warner, for the cover of George Shearing's *Burnished Brass*," says Silke. I was a naive twenty-five and looked a very naive seventeen. When she arrived for her interview, Sandy took one look at me, grinned from ear

Sixteen-year-old Victoria Vetry — photo/Silke

to ear, and leaned against my door — making her body into an "S" curve that put the Coke bottle to shame — and asked me to take her to coffee. When we got to Dupars, she ordered breakfast. In short, I never had a chance. Fortunately, she was a great model. Later, I learned she had an identical twin sister and was grateful they hadn't *both* showed up. If they'd asked, I'd probably have bought them a car."

Silke also worked with the fabulous nude model, Diane Webber. "I spent a day in a swimming pool with Diane, directing the cover for Les Baxter's *Jewels of the Sea*, says Silke. "Diane was a great underwater model because she somehow didn't blow bubbles from her mouth to obscure her face. By the time I got home, I had such stomach cramps from holding my breath all day that I could barely stand up straight. My wife, sympathetic to my pain, quickly put me to bed and began to give me a massage. Stupidly, I told her how I came by my trouble, and instantly I was on my own."

When he became executive art director at Capitol, Silke began to take some of his own photographs. "The first model I shot was Victoria Vetry (a.k.a. Angela Dorian)," he says. "She was sixteen, more than a few years and a whole lot of curves away from becoming *Playboy's* Playmate of the Year. The photos were to be used as 'scrap' for my first comic strip. I eventually gave up on the strip, but her photos didn't go to waste."

In 1960, while still executive art director at Capitol Records, Silke began to publish and edit *Cinema*, an international film magazine. "My ability to draw women," Silke recalls, "was getting better, and I considered trying

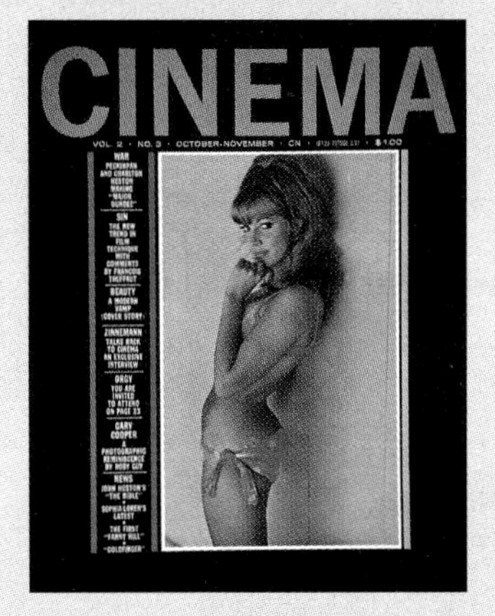

Jackie Lane — photo/Silke

another comic strip, but the process of reviewing films for the magazine made it clear I had another problem: I knew nothing about storytelling.

"But *Cinema* put me in a unique position to learn from the masters. For instance, my approach to drawing women came from a story that director Howard Hawks told me about Carole Lombard."

HAWKS: "[Lombard] was one of the most attractive girls you could find. And she acted like a schoolgirl. And she was stiff; she would try and imagine a character and then act according to her imaginings instead of being herself. The film was *Twentieth Century*. We were rehearsing the first day, and John Barrymore began to hold his nose. I made him promise that he wouldn't say anything until 3 o'clock in the afternoon, but I could see him getting worried. Well, I took Lombard for a walk around the stage and I said, 'You've been working hard on the script.' She said, 'I'm glad it shows.' And I said, 'Yes, you know every word of it. How much do you get paid for the picture?' She told me. I said, 'That's pretty good. What do you get paid for?' She said, 'Well, acting.' I said, 'Well, what if I would tell you that you had earned all your money, and you don't have to act anymore?' She just stared at me, and I said, 'What would you do if a man said such and such a thing to you?' She said, 'I'd kick him right in the balls.' And I said, 'Well, Barrymore said that to you. Why didn't you kick him? What would you say if a man said such and such to you?' And she whnnnnag-snarled, you know, with one of those Lombard gestures. I said, 'Well, he said that to

Sharon Tate — photo/Silke

you when he said such and such a line. Now, you're going back in and make this scene, and you kick him, and you do any damn thing that comes to your mind that's natural, and quit *acting.* If you don't quit, I'm going to fire you this afternoon.' She said, 'All right.' She became a star after this picture. And she used to send me a wire every time she started a picture saying, 'I'm going to kick him right in the balls'."

Silke remembers, "I tried to encourage that same emotional honesty in the actresses I photographed for *Cinema*. And more than a few had something going for them inside as well as out: Susan Seaforth, Victoria Vetry, Anjanette Comer, Begonia Palacios, Sharon Tate, Jackie Lane. The shootings with Jackie were so successful, I started a third new career as a glamour

Sandra Milo in Federico Fellini's Juliet of the Spirits

photographer for Globe Photos."

Silke's interview with Alfred Hitchcock, on the other hand, influenced *Rascals'* style.

HITCHCOCK: "I couldn't make *Psycho* without my tongue in my cheek. If I'd been doing *Psycho* seriously, then it would have been a case history told in a documentary manner. It certainly wouldn't have been told in terms of mystery and *oooooh, look out audience, here comes the boogieman*! This is like telling a story to a little boy. It's like telling a fairy story."

During nearly fifteen years of producing *Cinema* and then *Movies International*, Silke interviewed costumers, production designers, producers, and performers as well as directors including producer/director George Stevens.

"George became one of my closest friends, my guru. During one of our conversations, he laid out a formula that eventually set both *Rascals'* narrative and aesthetic structure. I had asked him how he got away with making the atmosphere in *Gunga Din* so exotic, you know, with snake pits, whippings, a gold temple, and such an unbelievably horrible "heavy." And George, well, he just kinda chuckled and said, 'Jim, look around you.' I did, and since we were in the Brown Derby having lunch, you know, with all the

David Weddle's If They Move . . . Kill 'Em *— photo/Silke*

agents and movie-mogul bandits around us — men ten times as deadly as the heavy in *Gunga Din* — I had to laugh at myself. George then went on to explain how *Gunga Din* was structured like a three-ring circus, and how it was prudent in stories of exotic high adventure to give your characters an ordinary domestic problem for verisimilitude, the example in *Din* being Cary Grant's and Victor McLaglen's efforts to keep Douglas Fairbanks, Jr. from quitting the army to marry Joan Fontaine."

Something French director George Franju told Silke also affected *Rascals*: "The source of beauty is a wound." Silke explored that particular truth in depth shortly after starting *Cinema*, as he began his long collaboration with director Sam Peckinpah.

"In a way," recalls Silke, "Peckinpah showed me how to handle dangerous dames. That is, providing they're fictitious."

Silke first worked for Sam Peckinpah, (*The Wild Bunch*, *Ride the High Country*, *Pat Garrett and Billy the Kid*, *Straw Dogs*, etc.) as the costume designer on *Major Dundee* in 1963. From that association, a professional and personal relationship began that lasted until Peckinpah's death in 1984. "Actually," Silke points out, "death is a minor distraction for a guy like Sam, so the relationship is still at play. *Rascal*'s Samuel David Breckenridge is based on Sam, and 'String' is based on myself, so he still has ample opportunity to scream at me."

In 1964, after Peckinpah had been fired off of *The Cincinnati Kid*, Silke moved from costumes to writing. "Sam was blackballed then, and the only work he could get was as a writer. But he hated writing! So when MGM asked him to do the screenplay for James Michener's novel *Caravans* and he was about to turn it down, I suggested we turn it into "Terry and the Pirates." He said 'Okay, you son of a bitch, but you're going to write it!'"

Begonia Palacios — photo/Silke

"That was the start of 20 years of 3 A.M. phone calls: 'Silke, get your ass out here!' I'd drive from the San Fernando Valley to his place in Malibu, get there about 4 A.M., and he'd start hollering, 'Don't you know what the first act is about?' I said, 'Sam, I don't even know what a first act is!', and he threw the pages at me. That's how I learned, by ducking scripts, coffee cups, and gin bottles. Literally! And, of course, by being rewritten by a true pro. I put a camel in *Caravans*, as a featured character, and when I got to the final battle, I was such a rookie I just couldn't bring myself to let it be killed. So again, the phone rings and Sam starts shouting, 'Damn you! Every time I'm ready to blow up the miserable camel, you've found some way to get the mangy bitch out alive!'

Lyn Silke — photo/Silke

"Sam, of course, wasn't writing a comic strip; it was always his personal vision of the *Heart of Darkness*. The problem was finding it. That's the story David Weddle tells in his new book on Sam, *If They Move . . . Kill 'Em*!

"It was a wild ride," Silke adds, "and I wouldn't swap it for anything! In those early years, we wrote every day: TV pilots, action outlines, screenplays. And almost everyone featured a nubile, brown-skinned lovely, laced with dynamite and laughter. The basis for these characters was usually 'Bego' (Peckinpah's wife, Mexican actress Begonia Palacios), but sometimes it was my wife, Lyn. She and Sam loved each other, but they'd fight like tigers, and he'd use it in a script. Sam saw Lyn the same way I did, and still do, not as a Jewish girl from Beverly Hills, but as an olive-skinned desert beauty. Sam, of course, who rewrote me even in conversations, added, ' . . . with a dagger hidden in her hair!'

"It took me a long time to get a handle on Sam's method, but now, in *Rascals*, every female character is based on some dramatized aspect of my wife's character."

Peckinpah also gave Silke his own brand of trouble. "I'm not complaining," says Silke, "it was inevitable. Sam had a strong narrative eye, and it dominated my creative vision for years. It wasn't until sometime in 1974, while I was writing *Here's Looking at You, Kid* (a history of the creative departments at Warner Brothers Studios during the '30s and '40s published by Little, Brown & Co.), that I began to find my own style and aesthetic. But at that point, it only applied to prose and screenplays."

In 1980, Silke began to write on his own, for Menahem Golan of Cannon Films (*King Solomon's Mines*, *Revenge of the Ninja*, *The Barbarians*, etc.). "I wrote over thirty films for Menahem, and every one — if I'd had my way — would have looked like *Rascals*. But the closest they came was Drew Strusan's poster of Brooke Shields for *Sahara*."

Book 3 in the Death Dealer series cover/Frazetta

In the '80s Silke added novelist to his list of careers with the four Death Dealer paperbacks derived from Frank Frazetta's famous painting. "Frank is an old friend, and I loved being involved with him. And I like those books. But there was still something missing. The problem was I'd seen Dave Stevens' *Rocketeer* around '83 and it not only awakened an old dream but pissed me off. Here this punk kid Stevens had the gall to put Bettie Page in a comic book when I'd been drawing her for thirty years. It shook me, enough to make me realize I was holding out on myself. That's when *Rascals* was conceived, and in one way or another, I've been working on it ever since." ❑

Cover of Jim Silke's
Bettie Page: Queen of Hearts